Remy de Gourmont

MOROSE
VIGNETTES

TRANSLATED AND WITH AN INTRODUCTION BY

BRIAN STABLEFORD

THIS IS A SNUGGLY BOOK

ISBN: 978-1-64525-047-0

REMY DE GOURMONT (1858-1915) was the most important literary critic of his era, and his studies of authors involved in the Symbolist Movement, many of them collected in *Le Livre des masques* (1896) and *Le Deuxième livre des masques* (1898), provided an invaluable map of its extent and a commentary on its ambitions. He became the principal theorist of Symbolism and Decadence, which he regarded as identical. Disfigured by lupus, he became a recluse before the century ended, and his health deteriorated steadily thereafter, although he kept on writing relentlessly while he could.

BRIAN STABLEFORD'S scholarly work includes *New Atlantis: A Narrative History of Scientific Romance* (Wildside Press, 2016), *The Plurality of Imaginary Worlds: The Evolution of French roman scientifique* (Black Coat Press, 2017) and *Tales of Enchantment and Disenchantment: A History of Faerie* (Black Coat Press, 2019). In support of the latter projects he has translated more than a hundred volumes of *roman scientifique* and more than twenty volumes of *contes de fées* into English.

SNUGGLY BOOKS

Contents

PART THREE: A FEW MORE

Introduction

*P*ROSES MOROSES by Remy de Gourmont (1858-1915), here translated as *Morose vignettes*, was originally published by the press associated with the *Mercure de France*, a periodical that Gourmont had helped to found, in 1894. It was the third volume of his "proses" that the press had issued, following *Litanies de la rose* (1892) and *Fleurs de jadis*, (1893), but those very brief works—the former reprinted from the May 1892 issue of the *Mercure* and the latter from the June 1893 issue—had been published in extremely limited editions, the former of 84 copies and the latter of 47, presumably commissioned by the author and distributed privately. *Proses moroses*, published in a considerably larger edition, which had to be reprinted in response to demand, was published in the same year as *Histoires magiques* (tr. as "Studies in Fascination" in *The Angels of Perversity*), a collection of short stories.

The title of the collection poses difficulties in translation that reflect difficulties in the classification of the genre to which its contents belong. Following a significant precedent established by Charles Baudelaire, such vignettes were generally described as "poèmes en prose," a label given further publicity in Auguste Villiers de l'Isle Adam's short-lived periodical *Revue des lettres et de les arts*, which used that label in its classified contents page for numerous items, including four by Stéphane Mallarmé, five by "Louis de Lyvron" (Louis-Antoine Duclaux, Comte de l'Estoille) and single inclusions by several other writers, including Paul Verlaine and Augusta Holmès. Villiers also elected to reprint the whole of *Gaspard de la nuit* (1842) by "Louis Bertrand," the contents of which he represented as cardinal exemplars of the putative genre, although similar items had appeared previously, including some by the great pioneer of French Romantic prose Charles Nodier.

The label is somewhat oxymoronic, the terms "poetry" and "prose" often being employed as opposed categories, a distinction even more pronounced in conventional application of the adjectives "poetic" and "prosaic," but that did not trouble Baudelaire or Villiers in the least, who were both unrepentant admirers of paradox and perversity. The genre also has blurred edges, it being difficult to distinguish many "poems in prose" from short stories and difficult to distinguish others from items of "free verse." There are also overlaps with narrative jokes and ironic anecdotes. Alternative terms were suggested as soon as Baudelaire's generic rubric began to be widely echoed; within the pages of Villiers' *Revue* Louis de Lyvron categorized some of his items *fusains* by analogy with charcoal sketches, but the term did not catch on and he soon abandoned it, titling one of his own collections *Poèmes en prose* (1897; tr. in *The Miller of Carnac and Other Works*). Another supplier of significant exemplars, Joris-Karl Huysmans, described the contents of his *Le Drageoir des épices* [The Candy-Box of Spices] (1874) as "*menus bibelots et franfreluches*" [small trinkets and frills] but that only added further to the confusion and ambiguity. Léo Trézenik set a new precedent by publishing a collection of *Proses décadentes* (1886; tr. as *Decadent Prose Pieces*) via the press associated with the periodical *Lutèce*, of which he was one of the editors, and Gourmont presumably had that book in mind when he chose his own title, but the intrinsic awkwardness of the plural noun *proses* probably deterred other potential employers. When Stuart Merrill published a significant anthology of translations of such work into English, he titled it *Pastels in Prose* (1890).

The precedents set by Baudelaire, Mallarmé and Huysmans helped to ensure "poems in prose" a central role within the Symbolist and Decadent Movements that developed in the 1880s, for whom all three writers served as important figureheads. In the novel that came to be reckoned as the "prose Bible" of the Decadent Movement, *À rebours* (1884; tr. as *Against the Grain* and *Against Nature*), Huysmans' hero Jean des Esseintes described the prose poem as the "osmazome of literature," osmazome being a hypothetical essence of flesh, which practical biotechnologists endeavored to produce in meat extracts pioneered in the 1870s and still familiar under the brand names Bovril and Oxo. He meant to signify by his usurpation of the term that artistic prose vignettes were a kind of distilled essence of prose fiction, which he saw as intrinsically "meatier" than verse, the latter being rendered metaphorically fluid by its employment of rhyme and scansion. Huysmans and Gourmont were close friends for a while, and must have discussed the question and the metaphor.

By comparison with the pretentiously lyrical *Litanies de la rose* and *Fleurs de Jadis*, Gourmont's *proses* have more in common with Trézenik's *proses*, which are light, sarcastic and satirical, but Gourmont is a far less casual writer than Trézenik, and even at his wittiest and frothiest his work retains an inherent elegance and surgical precision that renders his vignettes considerably closer in spirit to poetic endeavor and more reminiscent metaphorically of neatly-cut gems than meat-extracts. While by no means handicapped in his sense of humor, Gourmont never lost his sense of style while framing his jokes and he cultivated a kind of mannered laconism akin to that of Oscar Wilde. Like Wilde, he was always sensitive to a notion of beauty that refused vulgarity even in the discussion of matters that many other people considered essentially vulgar, which colored his attitude to and his literary dealings with sex distinctively.

By the time that *Proses moroses* appeared, many of the writers associated with the

Symbolist and Decadent Movements had dabbled in the production of brief items of prose, greatly encouraged by the rapid proliferation in the 1880s of new periodicals, whose inevitable space restrictions encouraged editors to show a certain favor to such material. A prolific reader and an assiduous critic, Gourmont was not only familiar with the efforts of his contemporaries but doubtless studied their methods and techniques with an inquisitive and educated eye. Several other contributors to the fledgling genre are included among the dedicatees to the individual items included in his collection, in which he also advertised his own self-indulgence by dedicating some of the briefer items "to myself."

It soon became evident that "poems in prose," in spite of their attraction to the editors of *fin-de-siècle* periodicals, had marketing problems. Although book-buyers had never objected to the thinness of collections of verse, collections of prose poems seemed anemic and poor value for money because prose was expected to contain the solid verbal fiber typical of novels. *Proses moroses* warrants consideration as one of the classic collections of prose poems, but it has to be admitted that the competition is not exactly prolific. The only writers who produced prose poems in sufficient quantities to fill several volumes with them exclusively were Louis de Lyvron and Catulle Mendès, but the former swiftly became an isolated anomaly as the length of his prose poems increased dramatically—when he changed his signature to "A. de l'Estoille" to issue his "epic prose poem" *La Chanson de l'alouette* (1880; tr. as *The Song of the Skylark*) the work escaped virtually unnoticed—and Mendès' collections, including *Pour lire au bain* (1888; tr. as *For Reading in the Bath*), thrived on their salaciousness.

Many authors did not manage to collect their prose poems, so that they only reached volume form, if at all, as addenda to collections of more orthodox short fiction or verse. Gourmont managed to publish one more set of themed prose poems initially published by the *Mercure*'s press in *Couleurs, Contes nouveaux suivis de Choses anciennes* (1908) but subsequently reprinted separately (tr. as *Colours*), but the format of that edition—including the erotic cover illustration—testifies to the problems anticipated in its marketing. His short stories, however, routinely retain a defiant poetic quality, very evident in *D'un pays lointain* (1898; tr. as *From a Faraway Land*). Collections of prose poems by other authors issued by the *Mercure de France*, including May Armand Blanc's *Minutes bibliques* (1902; tr. in *The Last Rendezvous: Stories and Prose Poems*), usually sank without trace, and "Saint-Pol-Roux," whose prose poems appeared in several mixed collections issued by the Mercure's press, quit writing in disgust at the poor reception of his work.

That near-elimination from the marketplace relegated prose vignettes to the outer margins of literary endeavor after the turn of the century, with a concomitant diminution of critical attention, so there has been little discussion of Huysmans' claim that it represents an "osmazome of literature," which has been generally regarded as a cynically flippant remark, as it was doubtless intended to be. Cynical flippancy is, in fact, a frequent characteristic of "poèmes en prose," very evident in Baudelaire's "petits poèmes en prose" and *Gaspard de la nuit* as well as contributions to the genre by Trézenik and Mendès, and featured more forcefully in *Proses moroses* than in any of Gourmont's other works.

Brevity, of course, encourages flippancy and a certain impressionistic manner; prose vignettes always seem to be brief in a sense that encapsulated verse does not, no matter how shapely they may be, and syntactical impressionism is more noticeable in prose. There is, however, a unique quality in the particular flippancy and impressionism of prose poetry, which is at its most refined in *Proses moroses*, whose various inclusions combine delicacy and sharpness with a particular artistry, precursory in some ways of surrealism. That combination of traits, and the variety of its deployment in the three phases of the text entitles *Proses moroses* to be considered a remarkable book, entitled to consideration as a work of art its own right, despite its slenderness.

This translation was made from the copy of the second edition of *Proses moroses* contained in the Internet Archive Digital Library at *archive.org*; it is undated but was almost certainly issued within a few weeks of the first printing, in 1894.

—Brian Stableford, March 2020.

MOROSE VIGNETTES

PART ONE:
A FEW

Matinal Distraction

To Laurent Tailhade[1]

IN order to exercise the most acrimonious malevolence, Primary, dressed like a rich cosmopolitan, came in.

"*(Affabilities, rain, good weather, as if bankruptcy weren't looming! Is this woman dissimulating? Oh, I can see in the clarity of her blue eyes the joy of resurrection, and immediately thereafter, in the corners of her eyes, two tears*

---

1 Laurent Tailhade (1854-1919) was, like Gourmont, a versatile poet and essayist, but was best-known for his irreverent satire and lively wit; his work was often deliberately provocative, and the selection of this dedication for the first item in the collection has a certain tone-setting significance.

that I've been able to provoke without appearing to. Widow's black dress, three little children. Aren't they nice, little angels! Was I told fifty or only thirty thousand francs? Thirty, but the larger figure, which costs me nothing, is a guarantee that I ought to adopt, in my own interests, for the absolute success of the operation.) I need, Madame, a few rings, loops, adornments, trinkets, but I'm rather difficult, not being in love, and ready, in favor of another, with no commission, you understand, for serious bargaining. I can't go above, however tempting it might be . . . (*She's hanging on my lips—that's the word . . .*) fifty—these are your children, three little girls? . . . in truth, three little girls . . . charming creatures—thousand francs. (*She's gone pale, put her hand over her heart . . . A deep, deep sigh . . . Nervously, she seizes one of the little girls and clasps her to her bosom, kissing her fervently . . . She opens the double-glazed display-case, her hand trembling . . .*) I only have that sum on me and I always pay cash."

"Oh, Monsieur, you're one of those . . . in whom . . . confidence . . ."

"Let's see—one last calculation . . . yes, that's it, fifty francs and nothing more."

"I thought I heard . . . go away, my poor children, go and play in the courtyard."

"(*She has felt the blow, she falls on her chair, she's suffering . . . oh, it's happening too quickly . . .*) Have I said anything other than fifty thousand francs?"

"Yes, yes, oh, pardon me, Monsieur, how stupid I am . . . You can choose . . . oh, Monsieur, we'll reach agreement easily . . . Here: rings, ear-rings, brooches, lockets, full sets of adornments . . . oh, I'm letting them go very cheaply . . . little trinkets . . . which will be, if you'll permit, Monsieur, a bargain . . . Oh, my God, where are you? Children . . . Mariette . . . ah! It's a slight daze . . ."

"(*She's pulling herself together, good . . . very good . . . as long as she has the strength to endure the experience . . . Capital . . . it's working . . . She's smiling, she's radiant, hurried . . . I'm sure that she'll kiss my hands wholeheartedly . . . Dear little lady . . . One could say that she's swimming in joy . . . She pronounces* Monsieur *as a lover does the name of his beloved . . . Bravo! There, I'll make a little pile . . . I know it . . . that's exactly fifty thousand.*) I believe, Madame, that this won't surpass my price."

"Let's see . . . oh, no, Monsieur, on the contrary . . . thirty . . . thirty-three . . . forty . . . forty-five . . . forty-eight . . . If you desire to go as far as the round figure . . . I'll also put in this diamond; it's beautiful and was once valued . . . some time ago, alas . . . at five thousand francs . . . and you can take from these minor fantasies the objects that please you . . ."

"Good, very good . . . as you say, we'll reach an understanding . . . Yes, all this pleases me . . . yes . . . yes . . . (*Now, while casting a final glance, take out the portfolio and put it away, several times in succession . . . Aha! she's had a frisson . . . good . . . a gesture that signifies. Definitely not . . . then get up abruptly and say a few polite words* . . .) On reflection, I'm not yet fully decided . . . Have the goodness . . . I'll see . . . I'll come back again soon . . . yes soon . . . put them aside, naturally . . . for it's probable . . . more than probable . . . (*She knows what that means; does anyone ever come back? Let's go, one more little shock* . . .) Bah! Might as well take them away myself . . ."

"As you wish, Monsieur . . ."

"(*The tone of voice has changed; she's going to weep . . . we're there . . . ah, there you are, tears! Two of them . . . jewels, true jewels, more precious than any diamonds . . . oh, how I'd like to drink you in a kiss! Are they not mine? Is it not on my command that they sprang from the depths of your heart, poor little lady, poor little mother?*) In fact, no; I have an errand to run . . . soon . . . Until then, Madame, count on me . . . and in any case, a thousand pardons. (*She's broken . . . she's truly broken!*)

"Ah, I'm outside, I can breathe . . . That ended up becoming too emotional . . . It's necessary not to overdo these matinal distractions."

The Partition

To Louis Denise[1]

A month in the country.
        Not in the mountains . . .
    Nor by the seaside . . .
    Where the air is bitter.

A month in the county, in a brand new château (old verdure, extensively patched, makes a tapestry there.)

Little Madame Doucin is looking out of the window; in the distance, the dormant

1 Louis Denise (1863-1914), a regular patron of Le Chat Noir, became head librarian at the Bibliothèque Nationale, where Gourmont was briefly employed; he assisted in the foundation of the *Mercure de France* but was better known for co-editing the *Revue française d'ornithologie scientifique et pratique.*

oxen are gathered in the moonlight. Not one is bellowing at the moon, but a few are ruminating.

Her Primary would be truly very satisfied with such a vacation-spot, her dear friend Primary, whom she has adored for three months, oh, a true Amour—not to mention that she will be able to write to her girl-friends in the ex-Rue-aux-Ours[1] under the heading *Château de la Corbeille, near the Clôture-sur-Prime* (a little stream with gilded sand—perhaps gold-bearing, who knows . . . ?)

. . . Primary, what a lover! What she loves above all are passionate, witty and indecent words whispered in her ear; that caress simultaneously the soul, the heart and the other. Well, for pouring such an enjoyment into her little body as tough as a hawthorn shoot and as pliable as a willow branch, Primary is unique;

1 The Rue aux Ours still exists; this is probably a joke, the erudite Gourmont being aware that "ours" [bears] was a corruption, the original name of the street referring to Oues, a variant of Oies [geese or, colloquially, silly girls].

Primary delivers. Thus, for instance, yesterday evening, while midnight was chiming in the neat white belfry of the nearby church (twelfth-century style, at least), Primary said: "Where shall I kiss my little friend to wake her up? On her hair? Golden, but not asleep? On her eyes? Golden, but not asleep? On her fleece? Yes, little friend, for your fleece is asleep."

Those are things you don't forget.

Tonight, the golden fleece, only the fleece, will sleep, and everyone is asleep, even little Madame Crocoeur, another blonde who is bored and is banging her head on the partition to distract herself.

"No sound: adieu the oxen ruminating in the moonlight. I close the window, go to bed, breathe . . . Hey! Someone's talking in little Madame Crocoeur's room . . . Ah! That voice . . . no . . . him! Him! Primary, *mon amour?* He's cheating on me and I can hear, and it's necessary for me to hear . . . Ah, Don Juan, I know full well that you cheat on me, but do it further away . . . It's really him, it's his voice . . . He's saying . . . what is he saying . . . ? He's saying: *Where shall I kiss my little friend to wake her up? On her hair? Golden, but not asleep? On her eyes? Golden, but not asleep? On her fleece? Yes, little friend, for your fleece is asleep.*"

Little Madame Doucin thought that she was going to weep, but she only pulled a face: the muscles of her rebellious face contracted, she wanted to weep, but she only pulled a face . . .

Breakfast. They go down one by one, scantly dressed; sleepy *bonjours*. Primary is there, on the lookout:

As long as she heard! Pale little thing, languid little thing, soft little thing, you needed a crack of the whip . . . Well, she'll have been stung . . . A few stripes—oh, that a single kiss will efface. I'm not as wicked as people say, oh, no, since I'm content to make them bleed metaphorically, poor angels!

Everyone has come down; they're only waiting for little Madame Doucin.

"She's such a lazybones, the little darling!" says little Madame Crocoeur.

She arrives, little Madame Doucin, she arrives, thinking: "I would have liked to weep, but I only pulled a face . . . and all night, that grimace." As I went to sleep I felt it coming back, again and again . . . As long as it passes! He'll think me so ugly. Oh, monster, it's you! And I adore you . . ." She arrives, she comes in, Primary advances and greets her.

She's going to weep! No, she's only pulling a face . . . ("But she has a tic!") . . . such a nasty grimace that everyone bursts out laughing.

Poor Children

To Henri de Régnier[1]

THE dear poor children of Our-Lord-Jesus-Christ, Primary holds them in high esteem, venerates them, in the same way that people in Bretagne bow and make the sign of the cross before calvaries, respectfully and deferentially.

---

1 Henri de Régnier (1864-1936) was one of the most important poets of the French Symbolist Movement, eventually elected to the Académie française under that entitlement, and his early work, sampled in translation in *A Surfeit of Mirrors* (2012), includes numerous prose vignettes and stories similar in their experimental spirit to Gourmont's short stories.

Humiliated on a gibbet, humiliated in the sordid baseness of a hypocritical beggar, the divinity of Jesus bleeds under either avatar and even—should one say it?—blushes.

A situation eminently incompatible with modern equality, for, after all, there is no shame in being a god.

Primary extracts the moral from these modest communion wafers, in which the Son of Woman offers himself incessantly to the spurious scorn of his ingrate brethren.

Yes, Primary venerates the dear poor children of Our-Lord-Jesus-Christ.

If, on a street corner, a filthy vagabond raises his battered old hat respectfully, full of courtesy, Primary responds with one of those ineffable salutes of the well-brought-up man, measured and discreet, offering a delicate smile by way of alms: such an agreeable hand-gesture adds the hint of irony that spices and elevates any banality.

The Dream

To Maldoror[1]

PRIMARY was nearing fifty when his mistress said to him one morning, with the particular expression that women adopt in order to announce to their beloved things of a rare and decisive stupidity, but things that crucify their own flesh and which flatter

---

1 *Les Chants de Maldoror* (1868-9) by "Comte de Lautréamont" (Isidore Ducasse) was sometimes held up as a significant exemplar of poetry in prose, and the splenetic character of Maldoror became an important precursor of Huysmans' Jean des Esseintes and the general attitude of the Decadent Movement.

them, things that they alone can say, things absolutely representative of their sex:

"You know, I'm pregnant."

"It's a daughter, Monsieur," said the midwife, with pins between her lips. Primary, his eyes vague, looked without seeing at the creature with the skin like a cooked lobster, the fetus steeped in amniotic alcohols; he was dreaming: a daughter; he saw her showing, under her eight-year-old's dress, the thin legs of a young ostrich, running and stopping running at the caress of a male desire, willingly climbing on to agitating, tickling knees; he saw her whispering and smiling, her eyes large and her mouth gluttonous, innocent and tempting, angelic and sly . . .

"That will do for my old age."

"Get away," said the midwife, with pins between her lips.

And when he had gone, she leaned toward the mother, more wiped out under the sheets than a hellebore under snow, and familiarly, woman-to-woman, said: "Don't worry; poor dear, he'll love her madly."

The Redemption of Ugliness

To Marcel Schwob[1]

T HE capricious hands of the Popp, all the Popps,[2] stood at midnight: midnight on the sidewalks and in the sharp eyes of pale-faced women.

---

1 Marcel Schwob (1867-1905) was one of the most important writers of Symbolist prose, whose short stories, including the mock-biographies in *Vies imaginaires* (1896), often border on prose poetry.

2 In 1879 the city of Paris commissioned a network of clocks, synchronized by regulated pulses of compressed air, from the Austrian engineer Viktor Popp, who had exhibited the system at the Universal Exposition. Some two thousand Popp clocks were eventually situated in railway stations, banks, theatres and mounted on lamp-posts in busy streets and squares, and remained operational until the 1920s.

"Midnight; it's done; I can go home."

As if slightly drunk, he walked, his limbs heavy and his heartbeats so rapid that the blood was surging and seething in his temples.

"It's done, I'm sure of it. I've informed them separately: 'Inaugural dinner, refusal inadmissible.' I've informed my wife: 'I'll be back at midnight, without fail, my only beloved.'"

He went up the Boulevard Malesherbes.

"It's done. Oh, it was necessary! She was so ugly! Eighteen months of marriage hadn't accustomed me to that snub nose, those dull eyes, that thick hair, that half-breed complexion and that far-from-slender waist . . . and those breasts, ugh! and the rest, so vulgar!

"It was necessary. I was ashamed of her. Oh, my dear Paul, you've redeemed her, and you've saved me, my dear, dear friend! Who, apart from you, would have acted with such rare, albeit unconscious disinterest? Oh, how I shall clasp your hands in my joyful hands! Yes, I could kiss you!

"It was necessary. Then I began to leave them alone, after exciting Paul by means of little tender gestures for my adored wife; I kissed Juliette on the back of the neck for a rather long time, then here and there, and I left. A short walk . . . 'Let's have a little music, then.'

"It was necessary. I went out, I'll go back without making a sound, and in the silence of the small drawing room, a sudden accord . . .

"Well, you weren't too bored? She, almost seductive and already not so ugly: 'No, Paul is so nice, but you're abusing him!'

"It's done. Juliette has a lover. So, she isn't as frightful as she seems to be. It's done. Oh, I'm not sorry. All the time, this evening, I was saying to myself: 'He's undressing her, she's smiling, a little serious, all the same; he's putting his lips here, and there, he's taking her in his arms, he's lying her down, he's coming. Etc. It was a difficult evening. It's done."

The capricious hands of the Popp, all the Popps, stood at midnight, and more: past midnight in the sharp eyes of the pale women.

Ring. Go up. Go in.

She was half-asleep, agitated. The lamp, not turned down, illuminated her breasts and her bare arms.

"Are you asleep, darling? Look, that little red patch on your breast, there . . . you always lace your corset too tightly . . . Oh, but you know I find you charming this evening! Oh, that gaze excites me! Just wait, little slut!"

He sang: "It's done, it's done, it's done!"

After a pause, he repeated, drawing nearer to the bed: "Isn't she pretty, this evening, the naughty girl? Pretty, pretty, pretty!"

And Juliette smiled, so perversely happy that she was almost pretty . . .

Yes, almost.

The Blonde She-Goat

To Albert Samain[1]

SHE was weeping, her head on her husband's knees, her delicate skin protected by a silk handkerchief, peeping from the corner of her eye at a letter that Monsieur Parietal was rereading, devastated. The young

---

1 Albert Samain (1858-1900) was a regular at Le Chat Noir, as befit a Symbolist poet heavily influenced by Baudelaire. He was peripherally involved with the founding of the *Mercure de France*; his posthumously-published lyrical short story *Hyalis, le petit faune aux yeux bleus* (tr. as "Hyalis the Blue-Eyed Faun" in *The Snuggly Satyricon*) enjoyed an ironic success as a children's book.

woman's hand rose, as if in a game of *pigeon-vole*,[1] making a swift gesture.

"But no, my dear, it isn't anonymous. It's signed—illegibly, but it's signed."

"Show me!"

Monsieur Parietal inserted the denunciation into his waistcoat pocket, buttoned up his cardigan and said: "Poor woman!"

Madame Parietal decided to sob.

"Poor woman," repeated Monsieur Parietal, and the blonde adulteress ended up sobbing for real, no longer having the captivating game of pigeon-vole to distract her.

"Oh, it's disgusting!" cried Monsieur Parietal suddenly, leaping up over his stupefied wife, prostrated by the impact, like a victim. "So, you've done that! You've deceived me! Respond!"

Madame Parietal got up. She came toward her husband, and, putting one hand on his

1 *Pigeon-vole* is a children's game in which one child reels off a list of creatures, adding *vole* [can fly} to each one; and the other children race to put up their hands when a creature is named that can, in fact, fly.

shoulder and dabbing with her silk handkerchief with the other, said: "Listen and understand! What have I done? Understand and compare! It's so neat, so well-written! Oh, I can tell you, I was gripped! Come on, you've guessed and you've forgiven me? My love, I've read *The Blonde She-Goat*, that's all."

"Ah!" said Monsieur Parietal.

"Yes, alas! I realized her, your blonde she-goat, your dear little she-goat . . ."

"Aha!" said Monsieur Parietal.

"I've done that, yes, but you dictated it!" (*Spasms and sobs.*) "It's very unfortunate to have a husband who writes such passionate things! Doesn't it make one lose one's head?"

Monsieur Parietal (*kissing her forehead generously*): "Ah, it's *The Blonde She-Goat!* So, my friends, I'm not entirely without influence on my contemporaries! Say, we're going out, darling. Oh, it's my *Blonde She-Goat!* Tell me, child, can you see from here the ravages and disturbance of bourgeois pillows? (*Kissing her forehead tenderly.*) "Ah, it's *The Blonde She-Goat!* Say, darling, put on your lacy dress, we'll take a carriage."

The Phonograph

To Monsieur Edison (of *L'Ève future*)[1]

COLLAPSED in his armchair, pickled in his bottle, wrinkled by the rancid oil of impotence, Monsieur Parietal blinked at the mute cuckoo-clock and, with a concordant gesture of verification, drew a sumptuous watch out of his fob pocket. He wept over it: "The age of undeniable small masterpieces is over!"

The valves of his mouth yawned; he humidified himself again; he became heavier

1 The famous American inventor Thomas Edison is featured as a character in the cited novel by Auguste Villiers de l'Isle Adam, in which he is commissioned to build a mechanical bride for the protagonist, dissatisfied with real women.

than a sponge left in a bucket; a mist like that in a laundry was blurring his spectacles and his pipe was dangling, extinct.

At the noise of a click issuing from the cuckoo-clock the valves closed again, a match reignited the pipe; a piece of deerskin cleaned the spectacles, the sponge dried out, the rancidity of the oil was mollified in the enlarged bottle . . .

Monsieur Parietal boldly dipped his pen in the bottle of Ink-of-Small-Masterpieces, and these words surged forth:

Lustful Sensualities

He crossed out *sensualities* and, with less impetuosity, wrote:

Lustful Pleasures

He crossed out *pleasures* and wrote:

Lustful Dreams

46

He crossed out *lustful* and wrote:

Youthful Dreams

He crossed out *youthful* and wrote:

Juvenile Dreams

He crossed out *juvenile* and wrote:

Infantile Dreams

The valve opened again, full of black pearls; the pipe fell; the bottle became a phial, and the sauce, so stupidly bitter that Monsieur Parfietal, seizing his fleeing energy by the tail, leaned over more ferociously than a crab pinches.

Arthémise came in:

"Oh, Monsieur must be in a state! I haven't reset the phonograph this morning! Dirty beast, more trouble than a child!"

And without adding any clarification that could make it understood whether the "dirty beast" was addressed to the phonograph or Monsieur Parietal, she switched on the machine. Click! A flick of the thumb to make up for lost time. "Sing, parrot!"

She slammed the door, while the sagacious Instrument said;

"'Have you read Parietal's last book, my dear? *The Demonic Varieties?* Of course . . .' 'It's exquisite, isn't it?' 'An undeniable Small Masterpiece! Very talented, Parietal.' 'A genius, even.' 'Yes, let's be just and admit it: Parietal has genius.' 'Don't you find his forehead impressive?' 'As the mountain that conceals the abyss . . .'"

Monsieur Parietal sang, emptied his pipe with rhythmic little taps, settled back in his armchair, peered at the nib of his pen, and finally, with a solid breadth of gesture, rewrote his original title:

Lustful Sensualities

He drafted seductive deductions under that heading, only interrupting himself to blink at the cuckoo-clock and whisper:

"Come on, my dear friends, treasure me!"

Xeniola[1]

I

To Jules Soury[2]

AFTER dinner, the pastor of Mensonges,[3] smiling, killed a few texts.

His smile was soft, and the texts buzzed around his sugared lips like crazy flies.

---

1 *Xeniola* means "small gifts" in Latin.
2 Jules Soury (1842-1915) was a professor of neuropsychology at the École pratique des hautes etudes. Gourmont took a keen interest in the development of the science in question, and could not know in 1894 how extensively Soury would ruin his reputation by virtue of his fervent involvement in the Dreyfus Affair, which began in that year and dragged on for more than a decade.
3 In French, *mensonges* means "lies."

With a hand that was still swift, he caught one, then another, and, in accordance with his passing whim, tore off the feet, the tail, the head and the wings, and classified them, rolled a little in the honey of his fingers, in large ex-pharmaceutical bottles. The housekeeper labeled those jam-jars.

"Ah," said the old Breton woman, who still conserved the candor and head-dress of Trèg, "Young people are coming to salute the Master; is it necessary to . . . ?"

"Let them in? Yes, I love youth (hup!) Oh, young folk are so amusing (hup!) Ah, my dear Anne so amusing (hup!) . . . They're sincere (hup!) . . . !"

(The old woman, moved, wiped away the saliva that was trickling like syrup from the corners of the sugared lips.)

II

To Bernard Lazare[1]

THE weather was blond and blue, weather of reckless (or culpable) Holy Childhood.

The dreaming Senators, the Senators of the Holy Prussian Empire, considered the embroidered backs of their coachmen, and the souls of those good old men were embroidered in unison with red eagles and futuristic lilacs.

Then it was the French senators who passed by—not many. They had a humanitarian and sterile appearance, and their souls were so scantly embroidered that it was painful.

1 The Symbolist poet and short story writer Bernard Lazare (1865-1903), many of whose early works, collected in *Le Miroir de Légendes* (1892; tr. as *The Mirror of Legends*), qualify as poems in prose, also became a leading figure in the Dreyfus Affair, on the opposite side to Soury,

They all ate together for two and a half hours, talking about others—those who had nothing to eat.

However, all that was pure symbolism; it was necessary to do something. They changed labels; the new champagne stimulated consciences, and the Senators started thinking, and one of the honorable Frenchmen, thinking too much, burst forth (his culture broth was populated by an infinity of intelligent and sempiternal microbes, and nothing can resist their expansion, even crocodile-skin); he was thinking about everything: 1848, the purity of his life, and famous and artistic buttocks.

He burst forth. His philosophical lips could not retain these words, punctuated by tears:

"Messieurs, a toast to suffering humanity!"

III

To Paul Adam[1]

IT was dark, the night of history, yesterday, and almost royal, uncrowned but in a black coat, as black as the night of history, yesterday, or even in a dream, he thought, he evoked, he said:

"Ancestor, my dear ancestor, my bloody ancestor, the blood of severed heads, severed by your signature, a sure blade, a prudent and decent blade, my honest ancestor, the blood of severed heads has stained my royal shirt, for I am almost royal; it is red again, from right to left, all red: O trophies! O dear heads! Dear severed heads! O examples!

"Ancestor, my good ancestor, my bloody ancestor, without you it would only be red

---

1 Paul Adam (1862-1920) published extensively in Symbolist periodicals, including a few poems in prose, and collaborated with Jean Moréas, but developed a parallel reputation as a prolific novelist in a neo-Naturalist vein.

on a ridiculous edge, my almost-royal shirt.
I've punctured a dozen female breasts—hardy
anything, they yielded more milk than blood;
useful shooting practice, assuredly, patriotic
and moral, but what miserable targets, they
only yield milk, ha ha ha! The May virgin,
nothing—an anemic buggeress! Two drops,
no more, leapt to my lips from her ruptured
veins—chicken blood!

"O trophies, O dear heads, dear severed
heads. O examples, am I, then, nothing but
a symbol?"

The voice replied:

"You're nothing at all. I, we, symbols of
this extenuated hour, extenuated and more
deflated than the secret glory of a callipy-
gian, we who died under the secular rut of an
obscene crowd—we lived; we were strong,
we were ferocious. Like a falling mountain
we crushed life under the weight of our
virgin breasts—and what happy cut-throats
we were, with the steel of our unbreakable
fingernails!

"Symbols roared then, even biting flesh; we drank all the old blood of France from the slipper of a Marquise, and we became so great and so vast that no stain marked our skin, and so solid that the infamous amour of a multitude of brutes killed us without dishonoring us.

"And we are symbols; we can live again, because rebirth is our right.

"But you, do you even signify the indisputable mediocrity of your century, for having riddled a few female bellies and a few naked bums of poor children? Ho ho ho!

"Let the shades laugh.

"Let the shades say: 'My good, my dear, my adorable necromaniac, you're not a symbol, you're scarcely a metaphor, you're only an obscenity."

The Tour Saint-Jacques

To Alfred Vallette[1]

THE Tour Saint-Jacques, solitary and ashamed of its outmoded beauty, the old tower of the talking beasts, beasts of stone and dream . . .

They indulged rapidly, that day, in a brief and instructive stroll: an American of distinction (which is to say, similar to all Americans, distinction residing henceforth in parity) and our friend Monsieur Virgile-Austère Méliorat.

---

1 Alfred Vallettte (1858-1935) edited the *Mercure de France*, with the assistance of his wife Rachilde.

"There they go," murmured the saddened traveler, "those old Europeans. Guarding and surrounding with railings a few deformed and obsolete stones . . . why? Because it's old!"

Raising his voice, he added, negligently, his hand raised toward the solitary and shameful old tower: "Naturally, it serves no purpose!"

"What, none?" replied our friend, in a tone mingling reproach, wrath and amazement. "Do you think so? Do you take us for children? It's no longer time for toys, Monsieur. We've learned to make the most of things. This tower is useful; it serves, Monsieur, the purpose of Science. It shelters, under the ridiculous symbols of its shattered rubble, firstly, a laboratory of experimental physics; secondly, a water barometer thirty meters high, an electric stylus . . . What? Do you see? Oh, that old tube, that ancient shell, that can't be a famous laboratory, but it's precisely that; it saves on masonry."

"Admit it," replied the American, glacial and mocking. "You still respect it, that, that . . ."

"But no," cried Monsieur Virgile-Austère Méliorat, almost angrily. "No, I swear to you!"

They passed on quickly, hastening their instructive stroll, turning their backs—finally!—on the solitary old tower ashamed of its outmoded beauty, the old tower of talking animals, beasts of stone and dream . . .

PART TWO:
SOME MORE

The Swans

To Ferdinand Hérold[1]

SWANS were swimming alongside the Louvre—two swans wearier than our hearts—and the current was carrying them away; two swans wilder than our desires; and two women were watching the castaways.

The soul of Bonhomet was floating over the Seine.[2]

---

1 André-Ferdinand Hérold (1865-1940)—not to be confused with the composer Ferdinand Hérold, his grandfather—was a versatile Symbolist poet whose collection of prose pieces, *Les Contes du Vampire* (1902), published by the *Mercure*, suffered the fate of many similar collections published in association with the periodical and is now phenomenally rare.

2 The various exploits of Tribulat Bonhomet, penned

Women raised their muffs high above their heads, like a signal of capture; children threw stones at the strange beasts; two mariners departed, rowing with fervor, and the crowd thought: "In a cage, in a cage, let someone put them in a cage, with a big pool to distract them, in a cage!"

The soul of Bonhomet was floating over the Seine.

Then, the woman leaning on my arm, squeezing it hard, whispered in my ear, very prettily: "Oh, swan broth!" And in her slightly sinister consumptive eyes shone a crazy desire for blasphematory cuisine.

The soul of Bonhomet was floating over the Seine.

---

by Auguste Villiers de l'Isle Adam, included a vignette entitled "Le Tueur des cygnes" (1887; tr. as "The Swan-Killer").

Paraphrases
(In the English manner)

To André de Gourmont[1]

EMBROIDERED with dawn and pleasure, how prettily verdant she was, the little girl with blonde hair.

The life around her was gay, for her, as refreshing as matinal hours in May.

No bumps. No chagrins, no scarecrows, but angels and fays, joys and bonbons.

"Maman, Maman! They've broken my doll! Her head! Her pretty head!"

The matinal hours wept all the tears in their eyes.

---

1 Presumably an obscure relative.

"Maman! How unhappy I am!"

"Don't cry, darling. Oh, little sad heart, calm down. See, it's nothing. Unhappy? Oh, if you knew! Don't cry, you'll be happy . . . tomorrow."

Embroidered with pale sunlight, how she trimmed and decorated the pretty plant with gems—future flowers—the pretty girl with such blonde hair.

The life all around her was as gentle and warming for her as the second hours of the days of May.

No fevers, no languors, no vile jealousies, but games and laughter, cries and caresses.

"Maman, Maman! They've broken my umbrella! Its handle! Its pretty handle!"

The second hours wept all the rain in their clouds.

"Maman! How unhappy I am!"

"Don't cry, darling. Oh, little sad heart, calm down. See, it's nothing. Unhappy? Oh,

if you knew! Don't cry, you'll be happy . . .
tomorrow."

※

Embroidered with gold and sunlight, how she
flourished as she blossomed with odors and
delights, the pretty girl with the blonde hair.

The life all around her was as mad and
violent as the adorable and regal storms of the
third hours of May.

No headaches, no annoyances, no vile
envies, but roses and pearls, hyacinths and
perfumes.

"Maman, Maman! They've broken my
heart! My heart! My pretty heart!"

The third hours wept all the hail in their
clouds.

"Maman! How unhappy I am!"

"Don't cry, darling. Oh, little sad heart,
calm down. See, it's nothing. Unhappy? Oh,
if you knew! Don't cry, you'll be happy . . .
tomorrow."

Sister and Little Sister

To Jean Lorrain[1]

"LITTLE SISTER," said Sister one day, with the soft eyes of a consolable virgin, "listen to me. Are we, yes or not, at an age for definitive revelations? Are we, little sister, you, blonde and perpetual adolescence, and I, brunette and precocious maturity, a couple of futile cyclamens, unpluckable and negligible?

"Answer me, Little Sister, by giving me your lips!"

---

1 Jean Lorrain (1855-1906) seemed to many of his contemporaries to be the cardinal exempla of *fin-de-siècle* "decadence," whose chief chronicler he was, particularly in his calculatedly perverse short fiction.

"Little Sister," said Sister, again, with the exceedingly dark eyes of exasperated virginity, "are we, little sister, you the girl with breasts as white as a month of Marie, and I, redder than a Holy Pyx, flesh that a tender Maman parades in a carriage; or flesh of which one shows a third at the immaculate ball of Princesse Unique; or finally, flesh at which men shiver because it surrenders for two or three times its weight in silver?

"Answer me, Little Sister, by giving me your lips!"

"Little Sister," said Sister again, with the terrible eyes of a virgin who is making herself understood, "Are we, little sister, you the bottle of dying odors, and I, the phial of strident perfumes, the occult lovers of a prudent whisperer, or the patient brides of a distracted groom?

"Answer me, Little Sister, by giving me your lips! Answer me, little sister: What if we were simply to love one another?"

Lot's Daughter

To Camille de Sainte-Croix[1]

PLEASURE emerged furiously, like an ardent red jet. Lot collapsed on the flesh of the oppressed. The idea of blood tormented him. "What mouth, or what wound of virginity, has vomited in my face?" The flood of vomit cloistered his eyes, sealed his lips and blinded like a mask the torrent of his breath.

"The other; she was called Mother . . . what a confusion in the generations . . . ! With the other, they went to pleasure with the trem-

---

1 Camille de Sainte-Croix (1859-1915) was a regular at Le Chat Noir, where he associated himself with the "Zutiste" faction, who built a successful career as a journalist. His sparse short fiction was never collected.

bling of saints falling into impurity—but Exultation, an exquisite phantom born of their breath, floated, head high and radiant, richly ornamented with fresh flowers.

"This one—when the mother was dead Lot loved his daughter, Lot's daughter—he loved with the sensuality of a chaste priest, he mortified himself . . .

"In vain."

"She was asleep . . . A little while ago—no, it was an instant ago, a single instant—she was asleep. She didn't scream. Her mother didn't scream either. Oh, she's my daughter, my true daughter—but what confusion in future generations!

"She was asleep, but she isn't asleep any longer. Obviously—and that's disagreeable, above all, because with what disrespectful eyes must she, at this very moment, be looking at her father, with what sly and—who can tell—mocking eyes, eyes spitting internally . . . ? If she were weeping, at least, I could console her. I have a desire to beat her!

"Ah! Now the mask is stuck to her face

again, and her bound limbs are agitating in an inferno of slightly excessive cohabitation. Her head, within the imaginary vice of coagulated blood, is broken like a bone in a dog's mouth—and Irony is frightened, as a murderer is frightened who wants, but cannot, being paralyzed, to repeat the *coup de grace* . . ."

He articulated, without external speech, his repetition of *pardon me, pardon me, pardon me*, to God, to Her, to all of life, to all things, to the bed hollowed out like a pile of sand trickling into an abyss, to the blonde hair moistened by the sweat of anguish, to the violated breasts . . . to the Christ of the alcove, to the copper Christ, who smiled at the lights so bitterly . . . to everything, to the broken door, to the gynaeceum troubled in its silence, to the mouth bruised by bites . . .

. . . To the mouth above all—but the wife of a virgin and now of a woman, the mouth of a child and now of a lover, the adorable mouth of Lot's daughter opened, and murmured in a kiss:

"I love you!"

Small Supplement

To Arthur Symons[1]

CONTRACT of irregular union.

Thus I am assured of days woven of gold and a truly superior silk. The documents are signed and sealed. Everything is anticipated, except the unexpected, a moth that slips and pupates, a worm that wakes up, between the pages of treaties. Part One; external and material life, that which eats and dresses, that

---

1 Arthur Symons (1865-1945) was a British poet and essayist, a contributor to *The Yellow Book* and *The Savoy*; he had to change the title of his seminal essay on "The Decadent Movement in Literature" to *The Symbolist Movement in Literature* (1899) for diplomatic reasons.

which shines, all worldly effulgences, that which rolls, that which whinnies, that which obeys, etc. Let's leave that.

On the contrary, let's return to the chapter of transcendences.

"You will love me!"

"I'll show you love."

"You'll be faithful?"

"Like a woman who knows the price of fidelity."

"You'll be tender?"

"An atmosphere of tenderness will envelop you."

"Obliging?"

"Useful."

"Ah! Pretty? You promise that?"

"I have, in accordance with the seasons, assorted creams, as for intimacies, Vesperal Breeze, Lunar Dew, Milk of the Matinal Gaze, Illusion Paste of Sleepless Nights."

"Will you have, my dear, tears of jealousy if necessary?"

"I know how to weep."

"And laughter? For example, he-definitely-loves-me-I-was-a-fool-to-torment-myself-laughter?

"My he-definitely-loves-me-I-was-a-fool-to-torment-myself-laughter is a pearl. You'll see."

"And smiles? I need smiles."

"I have them all, friend: the smile full of promises, the adorably pert smile, the troubling smile of the Sphinx, the smile veiled by tears . . . I have the sarcastic smile, the sardonic smile and the victorious smile, I have the poetic smile and the smile nuanced with melancholy . . . I have them all, I tell you. Without vanity, my jewel-box of smiles is quite complete. I even have the bitter smile, which is so rare, and the I-loved-you-before-but-there's-no-comparison-with-how-I-love-you-now smile. You see . . ."

Tell me—and amorous swoons?"

"Oh, I definitely. What are you thinking? But that's the B, A, BA! BA, BE, BI, BO, BU! Come on, for what kind of ingénue do you take your Beloved?"

"We'll go to the seventh heaven, won't we?"

"The seventh; I have wings."

"Tell me again that you love me, my Beloved!"

"My love belongs to you."

"You'll love me passionately?"

"Ah, as to that, my dear, for a small supplement, yes. I know the role. Gladly, but let it be clearly understood, PASSION is paid for separately.

Correspondences

To Édouard Dubus[1]

It is astonishing that humans do not know yet that their Minds are in a light quite different from the light of the world; but such is the state of things that for those who are in the Light of the World, the Light of Heaven is like darkness . . .

Emmanuel Swedenborg,
The Celestial Arcana, 3224.

---

1 The Poet and journalist Édouard Dubus (1864-1895) assisted in the foundation of the *Mercure de France* and was at the heart of the Symbolist Movement during the last years of his life, before being committed to a lunatic asylum and dying of an overdose of morphine.

HALF-UNDRESSED, he took her on his knees, and the play of wandering fingers signaled by degrees the localization of Correspondences. The tone of explanations: the affectionate irony that succeeds in capturing the attention of little children.

"But yes, darling, the human body, all of its internal mechanism, every gesture and all the organs are homologous with the spiritual world, with the Heaven-Hell, a vast space in human form, the Great Hermaphrodite, inhabited in accordance with its regions by celestial, infernal and purgatorial creatures; the infernal vegetate among excreta and dead things.

"The symbolism is not very complex; the angels of light correspond to the eyes, the angels of love to the heart, the angels of faith to the lungs, the angels of strength to the arms: 'A naked arm appeared to me that has a great deal of strength in it . . .'

"That resolute life misers enclose in the jail of the stomach; the dishonest wallow in marshes of bile; the stupid and the vain in the sewer of the colon; as for vainglorious mass-murderers, they expiate in the perpetual in-pace of the rectum the joy of the battlefields.

"Tender souls that adore children, and which make them, the womb of the Hermaphrodite will be your palace."

"Oh, how you're boring me."

"Here"—and the indicative contact was already there less tedious—"between the divine legs of the Infinite, is the dwelling of good lovers."

"I don't understand."

"Come on, imagine immense organs, and you, strolling, respiring odors of rut, rolling in the snow of seeds, picking phallic flowers; the grass is soft and frizzy; desires, like aromas, are vaporized in the air and the wind is singing amorous verses . . ."

"And you'll be with me?"

"Eternally!"

"Yes, but all that isn't true."

"Oh, child, everything is true. Believe—and also believe when I tell you the contrary of this, for it's necessary not always to believe the same thing. The route doesn't traverse identical landscapes. Let's be successively the dupes of perspectives that hurt our eyes; that's the means of avoiding boredom."

"And afterwards?"

"If you were a chaste virgin I'd parade seductive functions for you. You'd reside in the loins of the symbolic Hermaphrodite and there you'd see to it that the spermatic vessels don't extract from the blood, for abusive coitus, all its essence and vitality."

"Is that the end?"

"Oh, no, there's a lot more. But listen. My beauty, I'm afraid that instead of the delectations of paradise, our sins might destine us for excremental infernos, might smear us irrevocably, under the buttocks of the Great Body, among the adulterers and the sensualists, with the filth of carnality . . ."

"All that's very dirty!"

"Like life, my dear soul, like life."

The Crime of the Rue Du Ciel

To Alexis Lauze.[1]

To think that it happened in the street! In the street!

The phantasmal feuilleton was created there.

One sou, and one had the wherewithal to dream all day to the sound of the needle, and to enfever the bleak hours! The stitching was embroidered with gold and spattered with blood, and the fevers of the day emanated by night in quivering spasms of the morgue and the scaffold.

1 Presumably Charles-Alexis Lauze, the editorial secretary of the newspaper *Le Journal* in 1894, and author of *La Psychose hallucinatitre chronique* (1914).

It was terrible and it was good. Amour sobbed, crime laughed, daggers cut purses and bellies; it throbbed; it streamed. Oh, one felt alive! And the heart? To be loved as well. Ha ha ha! The lunch hour evaporated.

One morning, the sheets are as heavy as shrouds.

Nothing rare: one of those weaknesses suffered by the flesh of anemic girls with poor nourishment: blindness as soon as the right foot advances in front of the left foot; hands that tremble like a thin leaf.

The hospital? Oh, no, of course not! Rather go and see how far away the pavement is from the window!

The comrades of the quarter file past:

"That poor Adèle's eaten more bread than she should."

"To kill the body in order to arrive there!"

"She has nerve; she'll get up again."

"Plenty of others have gone the same way."

A week. Toward nightfall she said to Jeanne, who came in silently with two sous' worth of milk and sugar from her café wrapped in newspaper: "I'm not asleep, you know, and I'll only sleep one more time. It's galloping, pa-ta-tan, pa-ta-tan. There are two of them, my dear, the horses! Wait, they've stopped! Ah . . . !"

No longer anyone there.

Victorine opened the door.

"Come back. She's fainted! Try to fetch a curé. She's finished."

Two black holes opened in the white mask. A distant voice breathed:

"All the same, it's rotten. *And Paolo, pointing to the cadaver, said to them: A man in a blouse, who came in and went out through that window, stabbed the comte and took the seamstress away.* THE CONCLUSION TOMORROW. Oh, I don't want to die! My God, if I can only live until tomorrow, until daylight. Tell me, Jeanne, you can help me live until tomorrow? Jeanne, Jeanne, my little darling, listen carefully. When it's my last hour, my last minute, you'll read me, won't you, the last feuilleton, as you've read me all the others? Swear it to me? Say so, say it. THE END! THE END!"

"Think of your soul," recited the priest, as soon as he was at the door, "beg God's pardon for your sins. His infinite mercy is only waiting for a word, a sign, a thought of regret, an act of faith and submission to his divine will, to open his clement arms for you."

"THE END, THE END! I want to know. No, no, I can't die yet."

"Resign yourself, my child. Only say: 'Lord, forgive me, because I have sinned.' If you knew how good he is, how he loves his creatures, even sinners! Soon you'll know if you repent . . . you'll know . . ."

"I'll know, I'll know! Up there, I'll know THE END?"

She had raised herself up, her eyes burning with flames of desire. A wind from beyond life laid her down again, saying:

"I can die, then."

Ariane
A Modern Héroïde[1]

To Camille Mauclair[2]

OH, my friend, what adventure, what role
have you attributed to me, of all wom-
en? Abandoned mistress! An Ariane! Ariane,

---

1 A héroïde is a letter in verse written under the name
of a hero or famous author, named after Ovid's *Heroides*
[The Heroines], which includes a letter supposedly
written by Ariadne (Ariane in French) to Theseus after
her abandonment, immediately before her suicide.
2 Camille Mauclair (1873-1945) was a member of
Stéphane Mallarmé's Symbolist coterie, who wrote
poetry and short fiction under that influence before
becoming an oddly conservative art critic for the
Mercure and devoting himself primarily to non-fiction
thereafter.

my sister, will it be necessary for me to die like you, wounded and deserted? Against the lion-killer you had no other rebellion: Ariane is dead. A poetic and merciful fatality; my fatality is superior, a fatality of money, superior and modern, I'm modern; I can suffer—but I understand.

"How many times have you told me that one wearies of everything except understanding? I understand, I even hope, that it will release me from loving!

"*No melodrama* was another one of your favorite sayings, and how well you are able to hold your experience of practical life in that sponge, without any awkward effusion! On the contrary, a little reason, damn it! The quality of amour is revealed in the sensitivity of the epidermis, and neither men nor women ripen in the state of unique fruits of the tree of life. It's like a basket of apples: more than one apple is worth eating. One can find a replacement without even leaving one's neighborhood—a remark that is perfectly true but, in the end, doesn't alter the fact that there is a difficult moment to get through.

"For suppose, in the end, that I don't find one. What to do then? You're delivering me, devoid of thorns, to the cruelties of anxiety. Oh, my friend, this isn't a reproach. Reproaches are vain, I know that, and they squander minutes, the currency of time, quite uselessly. So, no reproaches, and let's respect sacred things. One does not oppose to an interest of the first order, money, something trivial, sentiment. No, what I am saying is only to distract me; I'm merely a woman, it's permitted to me, isn't it, to be a little frivolous? Frivolous! Allow me that and suffer, without shrugging your shoulders, that I amuse myself blowing bubbles. Don't get annoyed, I beg you; it's necessary to let children play.

"Ten years, eh! Ten years, my dear, that I devoted to loving you. I could have been glorifying silk screens or making babies, but I loved you, and I believed that it would last forever; it was my vocation.

"I loved you—which is to say that I lodged myself in you like a second soul, utterly convinced that death alone could expel me from that chosen habitat. I had no separate existence; I was a graft that lived on the sap of the tree, maintained flesh to flesh by the gardener's stick. Amour, what a poor gardener you are! Do you think that I haven't bled from the rupture? Here I am, fallen like a dead branch.

"In a few words, I'll tell you what I have in my heart: I would have liked to grow old with you.

"It's over, let's not talk about it any more, but be sure, my friend, that I won't grow old alone; for a start, do I not have your memory, and always around my life, in my definitive dusk, the ubiquity of your familiar body? And in the nocturnal hours, the revelatory gust of your breath, and during the days, the long days, the obscure and soft murmur of your words of old.

"There we are.

"You believe that you've abandoned me. No, my friend, that isn't in your power, for the very plausible reason that I don't want it. Will I resign myself to being, for you, nothing but a vague transience? No. You lived in me and reigned over me, a simulacrum created by me and crowned by me; kind, I haven't deposed you, you reign; lover, I haven't killed you, you live. You reign and you live, because I love you. Ah, what can one do in order not to be loved?

"Can you understand the miracle of my pleasure? You haven't quit me for a single instant, my dear lover, my dear king, not a single instant among all the instants in which our lives are balanced, not one—and you will never quit me.

"I see, I sense and I touch my amour. I love you. Listen: I love you. It's me who possesses you, me, the rejected and not the other, the darling. Poor darling! No matter, I'm not jealous of her illusion, but tell me, what if she knew?

"Oh, you think that one can recover oneself? What stupidity on the part of such an intelligent and practical man! You've given yourself, haven't you? Well, I'm keeping you and I'm taking you away with me.

"Yes, my friend, your precious life is at my discretion, and when I'm summoned to eternity, I shall take you in my arms, creature of my heart, and it's with you that I shall enjoy the profound and inhuman joy of loving infinitely in an infinite amour.

"We shall be in Heaven together, my dear shade, and transfigured together, my dear memory, we shall live eternally."

PART THREE:
A FEW MORE

Vision

To G.-Albert Aurier[1]

SHE was golden beneath her pale blue veils, like a Florentine stucco. When I expressed my astonishment:

"It's because I'm a treasure."

I replied: "A very elementary reason."

Then she said: "That's because I'm elementary."

---

1 Gabriel-Albert Aurier (1865-1892) contributed to various Symbolist periodicals, including the *Mercure de France*, before becoming the editor of the plush *Le Moderniste Illustré*. Much of his work was published posthumously by his friends via the *Mercure*'s press, following his sudden death from typhus, including several prose vignettes translated in *Elsewhere and Other Stories*.

"Who are you?"

"I'm the person you see."

"Would you like me to love you?"

"I'd like that."

She stopped with strident laughter my humble and amorous gesture of kissing her golden feet.

I searched the eyes of the golden virgin anxiously, but I only saw the gold and did not see the eyes.

Smiling, she said: "Try."

"Yes, I'll brush with my flesh that monstrance of flesh. Oh, how I desire it! Let me proceed."

My head inclined toward the golden feet, and immediately, everything disappeared.

"There, my dear," whispered the voice of the Distance, "what did I tell you? Gold, marble or flesh, I vanish at the proof of contact. I'm the Untouchable—which is to say, Woman."

Prose for a Poet

To Saint-Pol-Roux[1]

"THINK," said the poet, "think of the pallor of the abandonment . . ."

It is necessary to know that she wasn't young and scarcely pretty any longer—and amid the artificial blonde glaze of fine hair,

---

1 Pierre-Paul Roux (1861-1940) who signed his literary work Saint-Pol-Roux, was one of the most prolific and inventive writers of prose poetry in the 1890s; Gourmont could not know in 1894 that he would soon leave Paris in a fit of pique, feeling neglected, and abandon poetry for good, although some unpublished writings were said to have been destroyed when his house was burned by a German soldier who broke into his house and raped his daughter.

like an inflamed pre-dusk sky, white stripes were lurking, agonizing primroses amid incandescent marigolds.

It is necessary to know everything that the Poet knew: this as well, that the woman who was not young and scarcely pretty any longer had been cast off by a desolating caprice: "He no longer loved her!" Oh, even in a tone of great calm with gestures in the too-bad-what-do-you-expect style, that contains many sobs, and not so reckless that they did not rise resolutely to assault the poor heart.

It is also necessary to know that she said, after a silence: "Now I'm all alone; it remains to organize and arrange one's life," and that in saying that, she tortured her arms with unaccustomed poses—oh, still very beautiful, them, and even relatively superb, relative to the inconsistent youth—arms widowed of the very dear neck that she would have had so much joy strangling in order that it would not be pliant ever again under the embrace of arms other— yes, one could say it!—than her own.

It is also necessary to know that she had a truly gross chagrin in the pantomime of obligatory affectations—for come on, alone and not alone aren't the same thing, are they?— and that, if she had been alone, all alone, she would have sprawled on her carpets, drunk on bitter tears and *Oh my Gods* every two seconds, and repetitions of *What will become of me* and—for she was religious—*Holy Virgin May, return him to me!* in the intervals.

Nothing else remains to know except that the Poet had a great deal of wit and that he wrote verses about verses.[1] "Oh my dear, verses! Oh, such grace, such charm! In sum, admit that they're good. True caresses, yes, inexpressible caresses, caresses . . ."

"Think," said the poet. "Think of the pallor of the abandonment . . ." And the woman who was not young and scarcely pretty any longer

---

1 The phrase *vers des vers* [verses, or worms, on verses, or worms] is ambiguous, so this translation simplifies the intended meaning in a brutal manner that is not ideal.

became very graciously pale and finally—like an inflamed pre-dusk sky attenuating toward the candor of agony, all white, all white . . .

Oh, beware of consolatory poets, beware of the Word, of the magic of realizations, beware of Phrases that loom up and live, of improvised evocations, creative incantations, beware of the logic of Speech; all syllables are not vain.

The Poet said: "Think of the pallor of the abandonment of old solitary lilies."

The Operator on the Dead

To Rachilde[1]

I was next to the woman who would never move again; I was on my knees and I was weeping next to the woman who would never have any more tears.

I was weeping—internally, for I was too fearful to shed human tears—divinely.

Someone came in. It was an individual clad in black, elegantly, with black gloves.

I interrogated the intruder by means of the

---

1 "Rachilde" (Marguerite d'Eymery, 1860-1953) culti-vated a reputation for decadence with her lurid novels that was not reflected in her private life after she mar-ried the conspicuously staid Alfred Vallette.

simple gesture of a raised head turned slightly in his direction.

In a low voice, calm but almost urgent—yes, a voice that was almost alive—he replied:

"Madame, I'm the operator on the dead."

And as I understood—only too well, alas—that it was necessary to let him proceed, I stood up, moving away from the bed, my fingers still joined, almost clenched on my rosary.

He leaned toward the adored corpse—I watched—and folded the sheet back beneath the dead breasts of my dead love, and, applying his index finger to the interior border of the left nipple, he said:

"There."

He had placed between his lips the pin of dead hearts, the great pin, in order to have it ready to hand and to strike quickly

He said: "There," and with a single stroke, he pierced.

The face of my dead love was still the same; she was no more dead now that she had been killed twice—but perhaps her immortal heart was subjected, in the afterlife, to the transfixion.

Ah, metaphorical lance of the Roman soldier that transpierces Jesus every day, and you, mortuary rapier, are you not made of the same iron?

Then, with a smile of consolatory complaisance, he said:

"She won't be buried alive."

He talked about my beloved and held out a piece of paper.

I made him a sign: *On the mantelpiece.* Having deferred to my dolor with the polite assent that signifies: *I'm relying on you*; he went out.

I leaned over the adored corpse; it was a long steel pin with a burnished silver pommel in the form of a cross: a crusader's sword, a sword of Christ's militia . . . oh, the symbol is realized then, my love, since you really have, bleeding in your bleeding heart, the Cross!

Hell

To Louis Dumur[1]

IN his humble cell, traversed by strange gleams that did not come from either the nascent dawn or the moribund lamp, the illustrious Heretic was writing

At the head of his monitory epistle he had placed the undeniable aphorism, the basis of all truly serious morality:

THERE IS A HELL

---

1 Louis Dumur (1860-1933) was a Swiss writer closely associated with the *Mercure de France* in the 1890s; he eventually enjoyed considerable success as a novelist.

Now, in red-hot flasks, he distilled the filthy sulfurs, stirred pea soups in the devil's cauldrons, cooked the bitumen sauces, doled out the rations of boiling oil, steeped in resin for the anniversary illuminations the blonde hair of beloveds and the beards of lovers; he enlarged vast ponds of alcohol where fanatics were floating like slices of lemon in a punch, topped with green flames; he sprinkled with molten lead skulls resistant to the eternal Word, and the devoured flesh was magically regenerated in order to sizzle again under the immortal rain of fire; here, a terrible grinder made mincemeat of lying hands; there a rasp of superhuman mechanism scraped the sterile flesh of foolish virgins from their groaning bones; and hearts fell under the infernal millstone as multitudinously as grains of wheat.

The illustrious Heretic did not forget the souls furbished with the greatest care by the forks of fear, the arrows of remorse, the necklaces of anguish, the hammers of terror, the chains of shame and the pincers of desolation.

Then he passed on to ordeals.

He invoked sinister damned souls, lamentable cadavers during forth and saying, with eyes full of an infinite error: "I am in Hell!" Ratbod, the king of the Friesians,[1] emerged thus from the depths of the abyss and came to shake his red-hot shackles before his surprised officers. In the same way, Comte Orloff,[2]

1 Translating *Frisons* as "Friesians" loses the double meaning implicit in the fact that the trivial noun *frisons* refers to small curls, especially wood-shavings. The king of the Friesians named Redbad, Radbod or Ratbod, who died in 717 A.D. was notorious as the last ruler to resist the Christianization of his people imposed by the Franks; the choice made of the spelling of his name captures a double meaning retained in English. Legend has it that Ratbod almost consented to being baptized, but eventually refused, saying that he would rather spend eternity in Hell with his ancestors than in Heaven with his enemies.

2 Grigory Orlov (1734-1783), a favorite of Catherine the Great, who led the coup that installed her as empress. An anecdote reported by Monseigneur Louis-Gaston de Ségur in *L'Enfer—S'il y en a un* . . . (1876)

quitting Gehenna momentarily, manifested, thanks to his unusual presence in slippers and a dressing-gown, the truth of the Hell denied by an incredulous general. And others—many others—rejected momentarily by the gulf, marked on the living, on furniture and on tapestries, the carbonized traces of their fiery fingers, or, with a veritably demonic joviality, amused themselves, like the famous damned soul of whom the Venerable Peter, Abbot of Cluny,[1] speaks, returning to sprinkle innocent creatures with a liquid more corrosive than nitric acid, crying out in a voice not devoid of a certain irony: "This is the cold water with which one refreshes oneself in Hell."

---

related that he made a pact with a "General V." that whichever of them died first would return to inform the other as to the nature of the afterlife, a pact honored by General V. after his death in battle, who appeared to his friend in order to say: "There is a Hell and I am in it!"

1 The theologian and Islamist known as Pierre le Vénérable was abbot of Cluny in the early twelfth century.

✳

Clouds covered the sky, and the humble cell was traversed by gleams that did not come from either the veiled sun or the dead lamp.

The illustrious Heretic had inclined his meditative head over the table; he raised it suddenly and, seized by a dolorous snigger, he proffered these few syllables:

"And I too will go to Hell."

. . . And hearts fell under the infernal millstone as multitudinously as grains of wheat.

Prescience

To myself

Sol de Stella
Saint Bernard[1]

SHE opened her window.
There was a spring landscape, young
and unfinished, a landscape of belated dawn
and awaited gleams, of palely florid skies,

---

1 The attribution of the once-familiar Latin hymn
from which the line is taken to St. Bernard is nowa-
days considered to be incorrect. The opening lines of
the hymn refer to the sun being born from a star like
"angelic counsel" from a Virgin, and goes on to say that
it is a star that never sets and is always bright: Jesus,
conceived as divine light.

the inverse of an embroidered silk cloth, an embroidery of foliage in infancy on mauve tulle . . .

There was a pause before the certain exaltation of the awaited gleams. Something clarifying was about to surge forth in an imminent benediction. The mystic Star of the Sun of Amour was setting . . .

She closed her window again, saying:

"As for me, I'm waiting for the One who will never come."

Primitive Joys

To myself

WHAT do you want of me, shade of primitive Joys, and why do you return to obsess me every year, at the same hour, the last?

. . . Perfumes of sparse resedas and lindens, charm of columbines in mourning, fringes of weigelas! Freshness of clear streams under jealous alders, mint in which an angelic frog with the soft eyes is crouching . . .

"All this," said the Shade, "is also to remind you of the odor of hemlocks, supreme hemlocks cut in matinal verdure, to remind you of the hemlock and its exceptional and criminal odor."

The Chamber in the Presbytery

To Émile Barbé[1]

ONE could commune shamelessly with the sadness of grass. Under the thinned apple trees there was the languid brownness of dead grass, finally discolored by frost; the snow that had thrown the naïve insipidity of its sentimental rags over that desolation the day before had melted. Winter was shivering, stark-naked, and amid the black lace of leafless trees, a muddy sky was asleep, like the water of those haunted pools in which the cadavers

---

1 Gourmont had been at school in Caen with Émile Barbé and the two maintained a correspondence for some years afterwards.

of infants strangled without baptism float at nightfall.

He had just got up and dressed quickly because, outside the bed rich in feathers and wool, the vast cell devoid of carpets and drapes, with no fire, refused the offering of the most humble comfort. A hexagonal pavement of pink bricks that caused the lyres of wicker chairs to tilt and denied any rectitude to the white wood table covered in unbleached linen, where the urceolate flower of a Rouen faience pot stood erect in its narrow square container; plastered walls painted ocher with the unique attraction, on a platform, of the smiling Virgin of the rosary, in white porcelain, toward whom two lily stems were leaning, like innocent acolytes, in virginal bud, as slender as the immaculate penis of a child; the four-poster bed with a blue-green awning and curtains, parted at the feet and the bed-head by noisy golden tringles: that was the chamber in which the Friend was dreaming on that morning in December.

111

He let the thin yellow cotton curtains that obstruct seminary windows fall back over the tarnished windows, and plunged his icy hands under the sheets, still warm, like a coward.

That bed, of a coarse and heavy sensuality, appeared to him, in that dismal room, as a single sin in the life of a cenobite.

The Men-at-Arms' Entrance

To P.-N. Roinard[1]

HE reached the first houses of the little feudal town again, went into the narrow streets, passed under an ancient porch, which the rusty teeth of a portcullis still dotted and traversed that menacing vault, where monumental arcades and ogives florid with escutcheons were visible. In those solid ruins an inn was sheltered, dominated by the mighty keep, from the crenellations of which a thicket of ivy emerged. The courtyard was vast, enclosed

---

1 Paul-Napoléon Roinard (1856-1930) published several volumes of Symbolist poetry with an anarchist ideology.

by old deserted walls, only animated by the fearful cries of crows nested in the loopholes.

The keep, the ivy, the crows, the ancient walls and the ogives, all that obsolescence full of such a noble peace! He sat down on a bench, experiencing a real joy, the contentment of living, for a few moments, in the midst of tones that had seen faces, gestures and celebrations other than the avid faces, urgent gestures and vulgar celebrations of a mercantile century.

He breakfasted in the open air, served by a lively girl with brown eyes, whose bonnet, like a rounded miter inclined at the back fitted the ensemble of the vision. A similar waitress must once have captivated by her smiles the surliness of English mercenaries or halted, by means of a serious gaze of the same soft brown eyes, the heavy effervescence of Burgundian *reiters*; perhaps horseshoes were about to resound under the porch and lances would click against steel thigh-guards . . .

He heard the rattle of coats-of-mail, the grating of solerets; muted voices swore behind the grilled visors of plumed helmets . . .

A House in the Dunes

To Paul Blier[1]

ONCE, in the time of Anthony and Paphnutius, the Thébaïd would have tempted him with its caverns and its mute arenas. Almost alone, truly alone, in the disarray of recent mournings and the illogical survival of old habits—dead to everything that was not very distant, very elevated or quite absurd—he lived in a large square house, an Egyptian convent, its heavy whiteness crushed by the pale gold of the sands.

---

1 Paul Blier (1822-1902) was one of Gourmont's teachers at the Lycée de Coutances, and published a certain amount of poetry as well as a handful of dramatic works.

Terrain conquered from the sea, the ground had conserved its nostalgia; the grass it nourished had marine forms; it yielded underfoot as waves cede to the breasts of boats; and the pines, a sacred enclosure surrounding the house, were curbed by the eternal wind of the Ocean, like fleeing sails.

He imagined, on going home that he was going to visit his brethren in a monastery; he expected to see on the threshold the black robe of Père Hilarion[1] . . .

In the distance, the lighthouse of Alexandria darted a bright flame in the darkening sunset.

---

1 Probably the Père Hilarion who was a monk at Mont Saint-Bernard at the beginning of the nineteenth century, a former Marquis who corresponded with Chateaubriand.

News of the Unfortunate Isles

To Jules Renard[1]

IT was a mild country, sad and green, as if recuperating from an ancient misfortune, a vast plain, afflicted and resigned. I took a path confined between two thorny hedges devoid of flowers, with lamentable thorns that seemed to be weeping over the cruelty of their destination, and after having marched for two hours in the prison of the lamentable thorns I was stopped by a barrier erected like an absurd stockade between me and infinity.

1 Jules Renard (1864-1910) was an early contributor of prose vignettes to the *Mercure*, including numerous "nature studies." Most of his later work as a novelist is in a similar vein.

The brutally-squared logs intersected, delimiting narrow chinks of light; I looked through and I saw:

A mild garden, sad and green, where there were sad, tender and green salad vegetables, fresh and dappled, nothing but lettuces, and amid that tender pasturage, a troop of naked women. I was not mistaken about that for an instant; the descriptions of voyagers were precise; I had never seen women before, but I was seeing them now.

The spectacle interested me.

Woman appeared to me then as a rather graceful animal, which I classified immediately between the kangaroo and the opossum, but she differed from those species by virtue of a few very characteristic details. Thus, like the horse, women have a mane, black, bay or chestnut, which descends over the eyes in front and trails all the way to the ground; their hair is sparse, thick in certain places, brighter or darker than the mane; they have no tail; in order to scratch themselves they raise the front paw, unlike the majority of animals, which raise the hind paw; their udders are pectoral, whereas in the majority of mammals they are inguinal.

They wander hither and yon, grazing the tender green lettuce, one leaf here and one leaf there, with an anxious and searching air, sometimes sniffing for minutes a vegetable that I would have found very satisfactory, but which they disdained for another, similar or even less appetizing.

In spite of their anxious appearance, it seemed to me that they bent over the ground with pleasure, content to justify their material appetites, because for more than an hour, while I was examining them, not one of them raised her head even once; the salad vegetable, the good lettuce, was their entire passion.

Never, in truth, had any animals interested me to that degree; I would have liked to see them a closer range and touch them; I whistled, I called out, I imagined the sweetest modulations; as in the zoological gardens

I passed my hand through the bars, making appealing signs, pretending to be holding good things in my hands, but the herd was unmoved.

I was impatient and I became angry; I threw stones at the beautiful beasts, but my aim was poor, I did not hit a single rump, and the herd was unmoved.

However, I wanted one of those beasts!

The thorny hedge, the lamentable hedge, in sorrow at its destination, surrounded the garden with an ineluctable defense, but the barrier was not insurmountable. I mounted the assault of my desire; I succeeded, and the ruse of falling on all fours allowed me to approach unperceived a small chestnut separate from the bulk of the herd. She was seized and thrown over my shoulders; I found myself, after a feverish climb, on the other side of the barrier, without a very clear consciousness of that strange abduction being affirmed in my mind; and, troubled and frightened, not having got my breath back, nor looking behind me, I fled, glad of my burden, the good stolen beast—who moaned a little, but allowed herself to be taken with a singularly mild inertia.

What happened at home, in the little house that I had organized near the shore, while waiting for the ship with white sails that was to take me to the Unfortunate Isles?

Alas, I cannot say.

But as soon as I had deposited the woman in my enclosure, as soon as I had stroked her, as soon as I had kissed her agreeable mane playfully, as soon as, taking her head between my hands, I had gazed into her green eyes— eyes truly the color of fresh, tender green lettuce—yes, at that moment, as soon the green eyes of the beautiful beast, her eyes drowned in such an ingenuously animal mist, her eyes as profound as the idea of eternal spring, her resigned eyes full of an imperious charity, as soon as her eyes, eyes such as I had never seen before, were impregnated with their fluids—I became intoxicated, and perhaps mad,

What was happening?

121

Nothing that I can describe, since I was drunk, and perhaps mad.

But from that moment on, the beast, standing up on two paws, became very similar to what I was, dominated me and tamed me.

And it is now me who grazes the salads, the fresh, tender green lettuce.

And I know now that no ship with white sails will come to take me away from the prison that I have made for myself, to the Unfortunate Isles.

An Episode of the Last Judgment

To Charles Wiest[1]

THEN were judged those who had received the gift of intelligence and those who had simulated intelligence.

While the invokers of Satan fell like lead pellets into the excremental marsh of their own credulity, the favorites of Speech advanced under the guard of angels.

Among them marched a humble man.

---

1 Charles Wiest was listed among of the friends who arranged for the posthumous publication of G.-Albert Aurier's works by the *Mercure*, and his signature appears under a small number of items in Symbolist periodicals, but the dedication of this story to him does not seem inappropriate.

They were all judged in accordance with their works, and their works were so bad that each demon received his goat.

"And you, humble man," asked Our Lord Jesus Christ, "what have you brought me?"

"Alas, nothing, Lord. I have not produced a work, I have not written anything; enclosed in a dream of amour, I have prayed. O Lord, may I not be judged in accordance with my negligibility but in accordance with your mercy. You have given me intelligence, the Word murmured within me, but I have not fructified my intelligence and I have closed my ears to the sacred murmurs of the eternal Word. The field of your glory has remained sterile under my inert plow; I had the mission of evoking over the bare earth the splendor of crops and the grace of grass; the splendor and the grace remained buried in the soil confided to my genius; and while the oxen slept, lying down under the futile yoke, stung by flies, in the heat of the day, and while the sun illuminated the globe and gave it the essence of fertility—oh, Lord, what will you say?—retired into the shade, on my knees, with my eyes closed and my hands joined, I prayed!"

"Come," replied Our Lord. "Come, unique lamb who resembles me, child of my amour, son of the woman who made me a man, friend of my father, lamb like me and innocent, come that I may be your brother, and God will kiss your forehead.

"You understood, in the purity of your soul, what I asked of your genius, and the vanity of work and the wickedness of toil. Leaving to the sad the bitterness of sweating under the sun, you were able to attain the divine shade that I am and rejoice under my foliage, lamb avid for the coolness spread by the tree of life.

"You have received intelligence, man, you have multiplied the initial gift; I gave you a brain, you have made three of them, one on the shoulders and one on each knee.

"You prayed, friend; that was the Work that I had devolved to you.

125

"Ah, true and sure poet who was not, like others, a pimp of the ideal, who did not make a sidewalk in the unreal, who was not a whore of the symbol, you have kept your genius pure of all admixture, and fools have not drunk from your pitcher.

"Sealed spring, the water that lies dormant in you has congealed in accordance with the crystal of the Twelve Stones, and you shall counterseal, alongside the Angular Stone, the henceforth-closed door of the eternal Jerusalem . . .

". . . and that because you have understood that genius ought only to work for God, and for God alone . . .

". . . and here you are, innocent of the fornication of the spirit . . .

". . . here you are, charged with more masterpieces and more worlds than my love was able to conceive.

"Enter and be the joy of the Inconsolable; prayer has killed Pride."